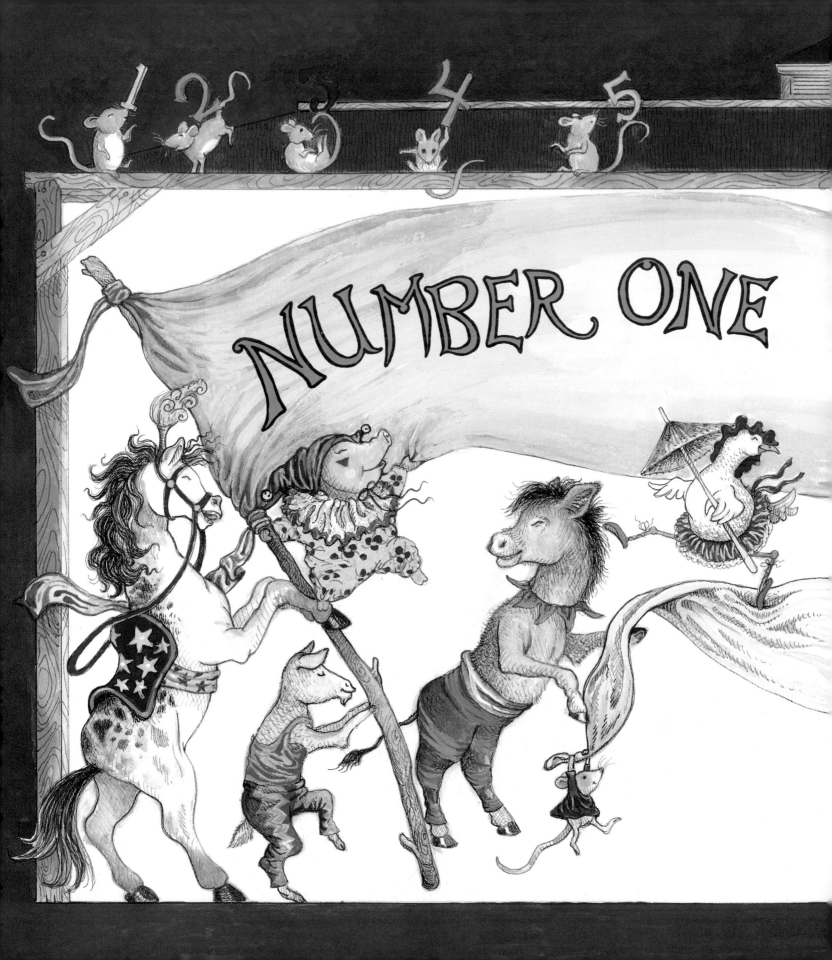

NUMBER ONE

NUMBER FUN

written and illustrated by
KAY CHORAO

Holiday House/New York

Copyright © 1995 by Kay Sproat Chorao
All rights reserved
Printed in the United States of America
First Edition

Library of Congress Cataloging-in-Publication Data
Chorao, Kay.
Number one number fun / written and illustrated by Kay Chorao.—
1st ed.
p.   cm.
Summary: Pigs, chickens, and other farm animals prance and balance
in piles, while the reader is invited to add and subtract their
numbers.
ISBN 0-8234-1142-7
[1. Arithmetic—Fiction.   2. Domestic animals—Fiction.
3. Stories in rhyme.]   I. Title.
PZ8.3.C454Nu   1995   94-9926   CIP   AC
[E]—dc20

In the barn a wagon stood,
big and bright, made of wood.
Out from under rolled a hat,
under that was Ringmaster Rat.

He touched the wagon with his baton.
Out pranced the animals, one by one.

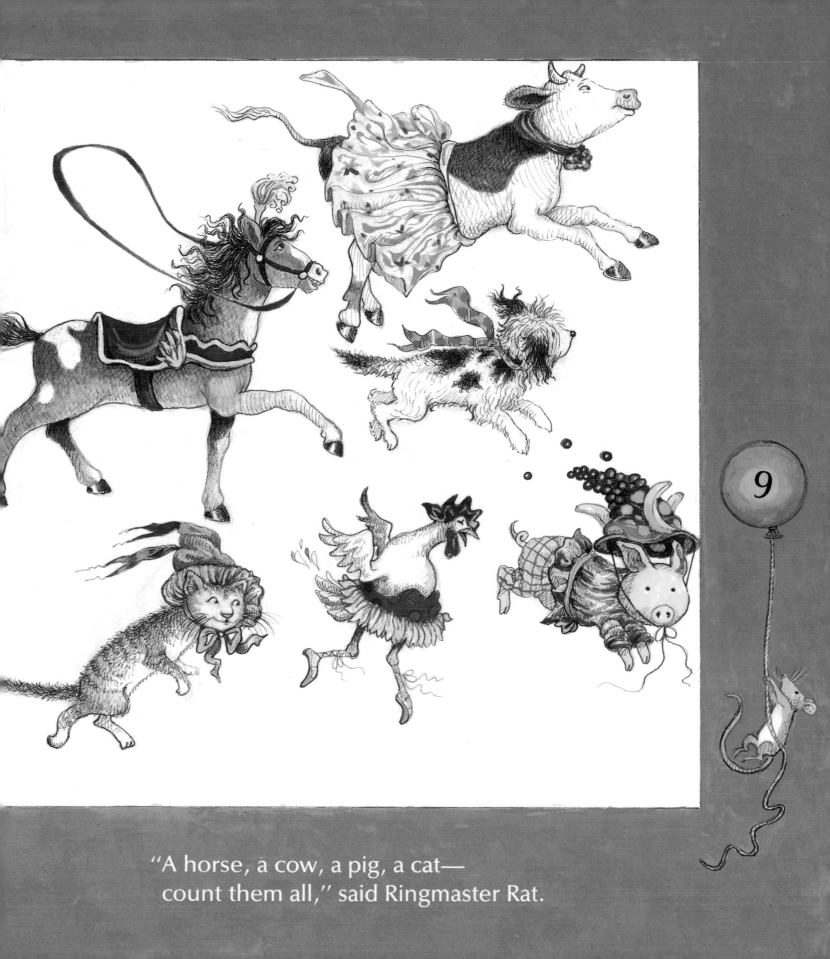

9

"A horse, a cow, a pig, a cat—
count them all," said Ringmaster Rat.

"How many pigs are piled in fun?
Add four plus three plus two plus one."

"If one falls off the pile of ten,

how many piled-up piglets then?"

$$\begin{array}{r} 4 \\ +4 \\ \hline ? \end{array}$$

"Four chickens on one side . . .

how many chickens . . .

four on the other,

balance together?"

8

"Two drop off . . .

how many chickens . . .

the others wobble,

are left to squabble?"

6

"In come the horses two by two.
How many are there? I know, do you?"

4
+6
———
?

10

"Four circus dogs join six horses prancing.
How many dogs and horses dancing?"

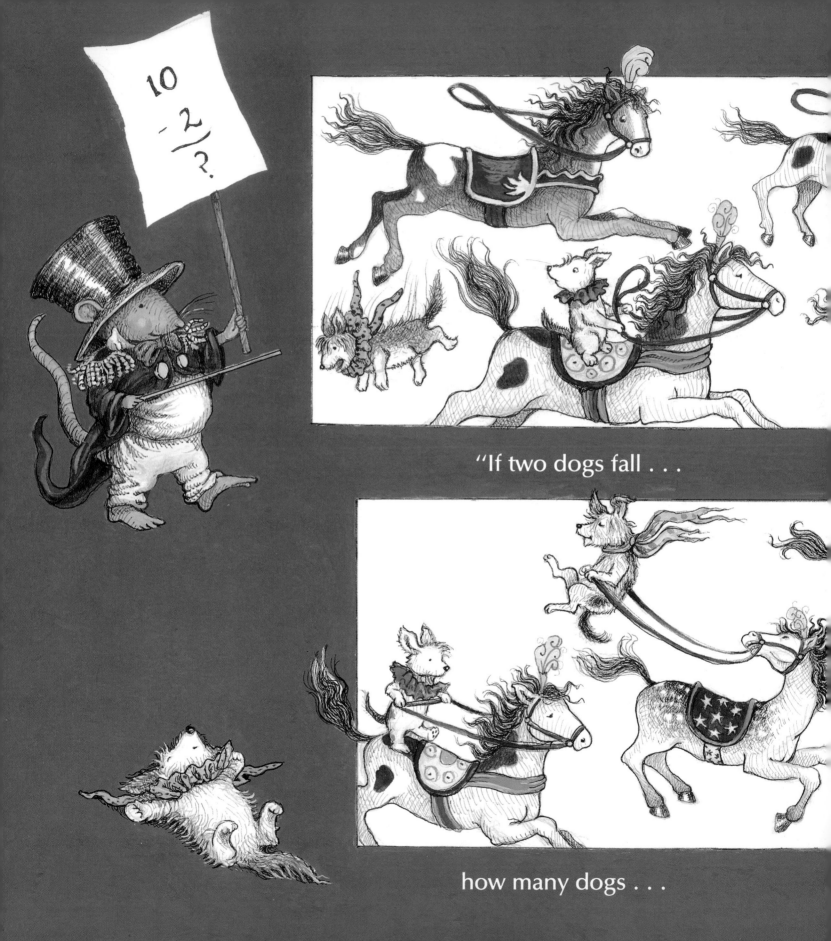

"If two dogs fall . . .

how many dogs . . .

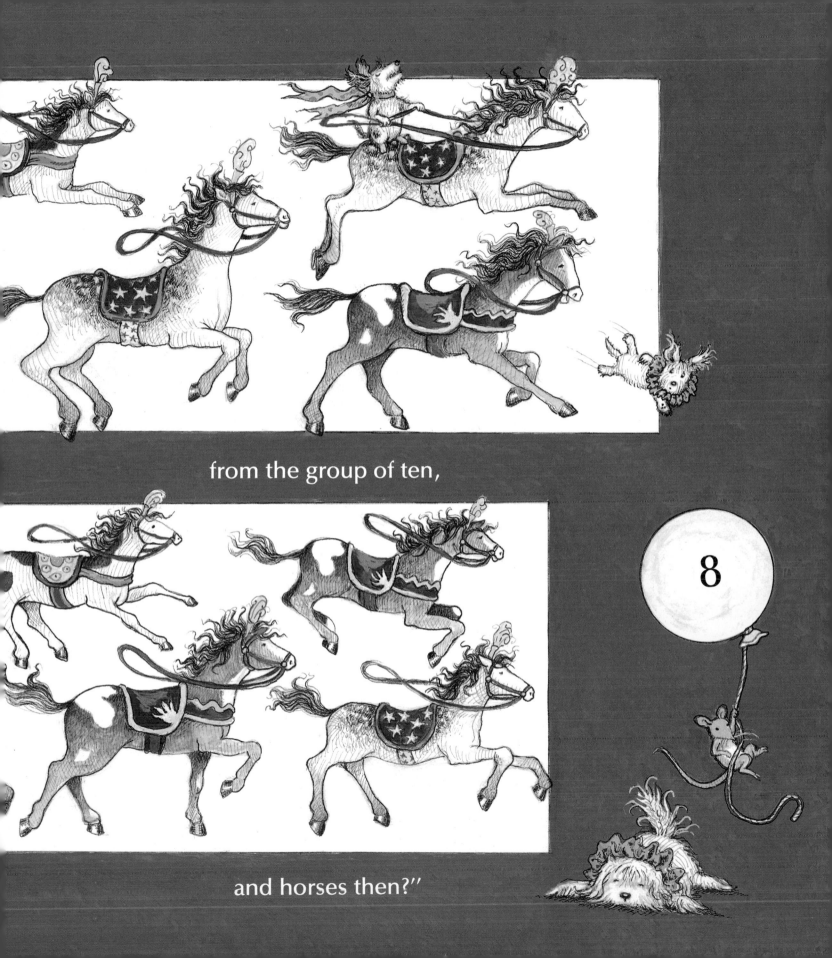

from the group of ten,

and horses then?"

8

5
+4
?

"Five tumbling mice join four cycling cats.

How many mice and cats wearing hats?"

9

"Ten in a car, including a cow.

10
−3
?

7

Three fall off. How many now?"

"Three goats and three donkeys fly through the air.

How many together are swinging there?"

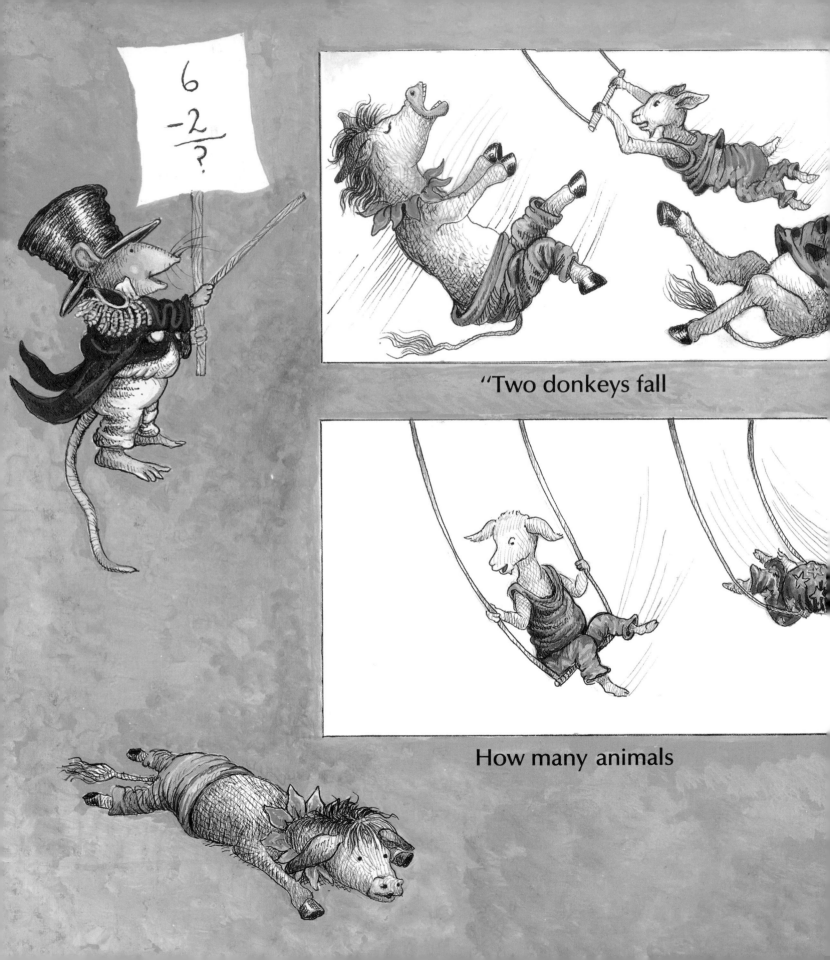

$$\begin{array}{r} 6 \\ -2 \\ \hline ? \end{array}$$

"Two donkeys fall

How many animals

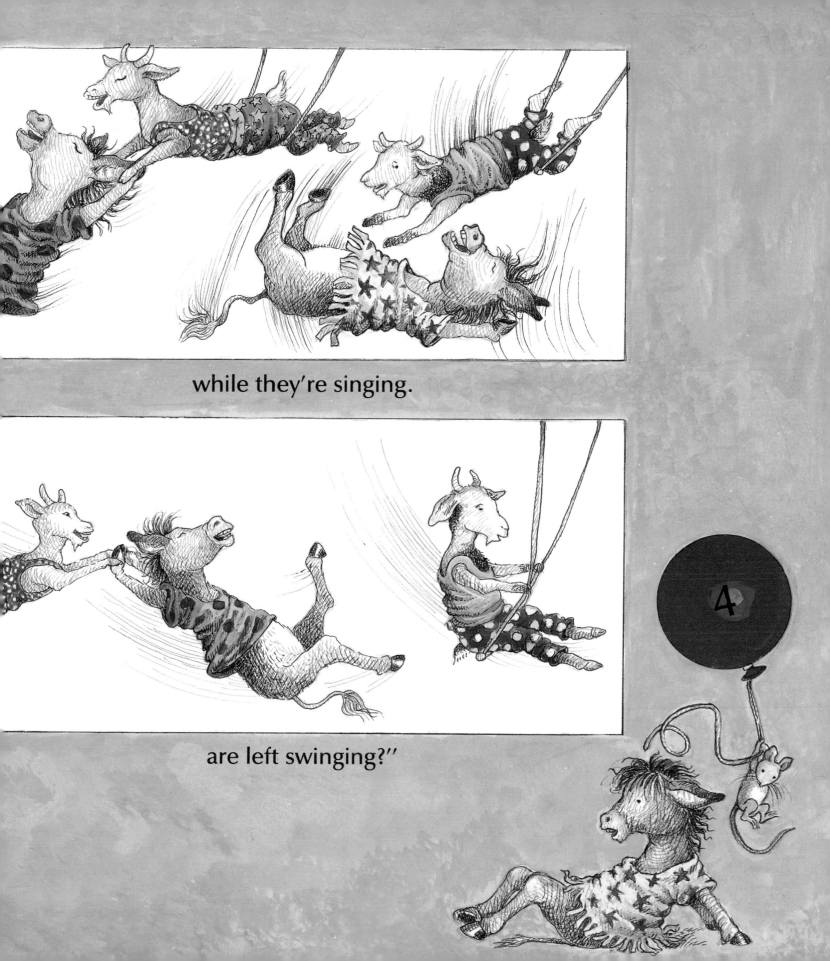

while they're singing.

are left swinging?"

4

"Back to the wagon one by one,
count the animals as they run."

Ringmaster Rat bows down low.
"I hope you all enjoyed our show."

$$4+3+2+1=10$$

$$1+1+1+1+1+1+1+1=9$$

$$10-1=9 \qquad 4+4=8 \qquad 8-2=6 \qquad 2+2+2=6$$

$$10-2=8 \qquad 5+4=9$$

$$4+6=10$$

$$10-3=7 \qquad 3+3=6 \qquad 6-2=4$$

$$1+1+1+1+1+1+1+1+1=9$$